About the Author

Linda Flashinski is a retired educator and freelance writer who has published two books of her columns, *In What Light There Is* and *A Journey Through the Seasons*, along with numerous writings which have appeared in various magazines and publications. She has also worked as a radio host. She lives in Caledonia, Wisconsin with her husband, and is a devoted mother and grandmother.

Prairie Voices
A Journey Westward

Linda Clare Flashinski
———————————

Prairie Voices
A Journey Westward

Olympia Publishers
London

www.olympiapublishers.com
OLYMPIA PAPERBACK EDITION

Copyright © Linda Clare Flashinski 2022
Cover illustration by Jerrold Belland

The right of Linda Clare Flashinski to be identified as author of this work has been asserted in accordance with sections 77 and 78 of the Copyright, Designs and Patents Act 1988.

All Rights Reserved

No reproduction, copy or transmission of this publication may be made without written permission.
No paragraph of this publication may be reproduced, copied or transmitted save with the written permission of the publisher, or in accordance with the provisions of the Copyright Act 1956 (as amended).

Any person who commits any unauthorised act in relation to this publication may be liable to criminal prosecution and civil claims for damage.

A CIP catalogue record for this title is available from the British Library.

ISBN: 978-1-80074-192-8

This is a work of fiction.
Names, characters, places and incidents originate from the writer's imagination. Any resemblance to actual persons, living or dead, is purely coincidental.

First Published in 2022

Olympia Publishers
Tallis House
2 Tallis Street
London
EC4Y 0AB

Printed in Great Britain

Dedication

Dedicated to all who travel on paths rich with both joys and struggles. May we be deepened by our journeys toward becoming kinder, gentler people.

Acknowledgements

Over the years, many family members and friends have helped me on my writing journey. To all who have encouraged and enlightened me, my deepest gratitude.

To the Reader

"Of what alchemy we are made. Let us, while here, understand one another. That is a divine gift."
– Jane Patricia McCarthy, ancestor of the author

As an author, I have been so fortunate to have had an ancestor who wrote words like those above about her ancestors who traveled across the country after the Great Chicago Fire of 1871. This fire was, ironically, the same date as the Peshtigo, Wisconsin fire that killed many more people than the Chicago fire did. But that is a story for a different time. Ever since I read the words of Jane Patricia McCarthy, I have wanted to put together a book for young people encapsulating the feelings, the hardships, and the joys of that amazing journey in that amazing time. The result is the book you are now reading.

This book, while based on a letter of my ancestor, is a work of fiction. I used names from our ancestry as both the Toner and the Harwood names were ancestral names for me. But the names and ages of the parents and children are fictional. I didn't want to create a factual dialogue, but instead I wished to convey some of the hardships they endured and some of the emotions they must have carried within themselves.

As Jane McCarthy wrote of her ancestors, "Let us keep their memory, forgetting all the mistakes, and in your life, let my remembrance linger, not as a ghost that haunts you, but as something precious to remember."

And so I send this book out to you, remembering those who have gone before us "as something precious to remember." I hope you will find some preciousness in my words, as I have found in hers.

Great journeys to you.

Linda Clare Flashinski

The Toner Family, 1872
Samuel Toner, Father
Mary Toner, Mother

Children
Joseph Toner, 18 years old
Elizabeth Toner, 17 years old
Jeremy Toner, 13 years old
Peter Toner, 10 years old
Alma Toner, 7 years old
Benjamin Toner, Deceased 1871
at the age of 37 months
Jennifer Toner, 10 months

Harwood Family Travelling with Toners in Separate Wagon
Jonah Harwood, Father
Rebecca, Mother

Children
John Harwood, 18 years old
Abby Harwood, 12 years old
Emily Harwood, 4 years old

PART I
TRAVELLING...

Papa

To live is to journey.
From the fires of Chicago
that threatened our farm
we move now
to new land marked for farmers.
Yet still I wonder at having dragged them all so far,
baby Jenny just an infant,
and Mary nursing her still,
hoping the milk will keep her strong.
Mary was pale tonight,
and her fingers trembled
when she poured the lemon water for the children.
She does too much,
but there is much to do.

Have I asked too great a thing of them?

Mama

Perhaps our children's children will think of us,
of the long, bumpy trail
that led us from the fires of Chicago
to the western prairies.

Perhaps our children's children will talk of us,
of the worry and the sameness of our days,
of moving about in the dry dusts of this summer.

Perhaps our children's children will guess of us,
of the tearing from the place
where Benny was a boy, still with us.

Perhaps our children's children will think of us
in the many, many years yet to come.

Elizabeth

I tire these days,
tire of being a daughter of the westward wagons,
long days of bumpity-bump,
bumpity-bump
along endless paths
that push the dust into bonnets
and fingernails
and nostrils.

I tire of the work,
the wash-clean-feed cycle of our lives.
I tire of the illness, like the fever that took Benny.
I tire of the monotony of long days,
All the same.
All the same.

And mostly, I tire of the dirt that bathes us
on these dry, dry days.

Joseph

My banjo's voice is silenced now,
packed away in the wagon amidst the other boxes,
preserved food, extra blankets, towels.

I miss the solitude of music
that lets me learn its ways.

It would be good to have a home
for music once again.

Alma and Mama

Alma:
"I pretend I am Princess Isabella
and we are riding through dangerous trails
to a perfect kingdom."

Mama:
"Then I am glad, so glad
that you can pretend."

Alma and Elizabeth

Alma:
"Braid my golden tresses, Elizabeth,
to look like the princess in my fairy tale."

Elizabeth:
"You don't have golden tresses,
just brownish hair like mine."

Alma:
"But I wish to look like Isabella
in my fairy tale."

Elizabeth:
"We are not princesses, Alma,
and this is not a fairy tale."

Mama

To wonder is to be a mother.
Perhaps if I had nursed Ben a little longer
he could have fought the fever
that pulled him under.
But he was over two
and it seemed time for him to move away from nursing,
away from baby things.

Yet, perhaps,
if I had nursed him a little longer…

Papa

My legs cramp up,
only one break a day to stretch them.
Even at night when we stop,
we sleep in the wagon
to be protected from
the bugs and elements.

After this journey,
I will always look differently
at animals, caged.

Jeremy

When we stopped today to run awhile,
there was a cloud
that looked like a child
blowing bubbles upward.
Mama was washing clothes
and gave us soap for bubbles,
and we chased them through the fields.
One bubble popped against a bird
who shook himself dry,
looking down indignantly,
from the throne of his branch.

Mama

When we were married,
they told me that,
with Samuel's hair,
I would be blessed with many red-haired children.
But only Benjamin was truly red-headed
and busy like his father.
His grin was Samuel's, too,
a younger version.

Samuel doesn't smile the way he did
in those days when he carried Benny,
laughing, on his shoulders.

Joseph

The woods is the only place
where I can sketch.
It is so difficult
in the moving wagon.
I am like a bird,
its leg caught in a branch
who continues to try to fly.

Alma

There are no girls my age to play with.
I remember jumping rope in the schoolyard.

"Hoppity-bump,
Rickety-thump.
Two feet.
One foot.
JUMP, JUMP, JUMP!"

Sarah Margaret always teased
that I played the game wrong,
and told the girls that I was too little.
But Mama said not to mind her,
that people who make such unhappiness
have great sorrows of their own.

Today, I would be happy even
to see Sarah Margaret.

Mama

I nurse you, little Jenny,
and your fingers curl on mine.

It is a hard life here,
not so gentle as your fingers
or your falling-into-sleep smile.
It is a hard life here,
for women especially.
We women do not rest
between the cycles of clean,
wash, feed, mend.
We do not rest
except to nurse a baby
or hold a sickly child.

You should have been a boy
to keep your hurt inside,
and toughen young.
We live a hard life, little Jenny.
We prairie women
lead a hard, hard life.

Papa

How Jeremy and Peter love to run and be outdoors.
The long days of riding
have taken the flush from their faces,
and they need a home for running days,
                and fishing days,
                          and hunting days,
and days to grow as strong and tall as trees.

They will have the strength of prairie men.

Joseph

It could have been that I was not my father's son.
He laughs so strong and hard,
and he doesn't flinch to skin the autumn deer.
He keeps his words inside.
If I didn't see their love so clear,
I would think I could have been
another father's son.

Papa

Of what strange alchemy we are made.

I could have whittled Joseph into a tougher fiber,
could have from early on turned him away from his music
and drawing
into pursuits that would help him in this prairie life,
        planting, fishing, hunting.
He thinks I do not see his wince
when we drag in the new-killed deer.
Yet his face was always gentler than the others,
        with the softness of a poet,
        the quiet of his mother.
It would have been as if to tie a tree
to force the branches growth
to all one side.
        It did not seem what nature had intended.

Yet still I see his face
so given up to drawing,
and I wonder…
        Is there a place on the prairie
        for a boy who draws and sings?

Joseph

The canvas over the wagon
began to leak in the night
during the storms that pummeled us.
This prairie trip has been so quiet, so dry,
like old parchment paper in flames, Papa said.
Until tonight.
The pounding started
more fearful than the dusty quiet had been.
I slept, finally,
'til Papa shook me.
"The canvas top is leaking, son.
The youngsters will get chilled,
and come down ill again.
We must find out now
what there is to do."

There is a lurking fear here
in what could be,
always a possible enemy ahead,
blocking our way,
stalling our progress.
Still we trudge on daily,
wishing fate to let us be.

Papa and I,
late into the night,
patched and sealed and tightened every spoke.
And at the end only,
"We have done well, son. Go back to sleep."

The leak we fixed, finally.
The ghosts that haunt us,
we did not.

Mama

There are days I would just like
to have curtains again,
blue checks on white
over my dishpans.

Such simple things remembered
when you wander,
day after day,
nomads in the dust.

Alma

    Rumble,
      Rumble,
        wagon wheels.
Darkness comes,
    and nighttime steals.

    Rattle,
      Rattle,
        wagon spokes.
Dragons come
    with fire and smoke.

    Hurry,
      Hurry,
        wagon, steer
the princess to her kingdom near.

    Rumble,
      Rumble,
        wagon wheels.

Darkness comes,
and nighttime steals.

Jeremy and Joseph

Jeremy:
"Once your banjo is back, Joseph,
you should make a song
of the rumbling of the wheels."

Joseph:
"I think, in days yet to come,
every song I make
will be full
of the rumbling of the wheels."

Papa

My back is sore with driving,
and aches like a hammered thumb.
How long 'til we arrive?
How long 'til we arrive?

Mama

Bones get tired like people
when they're cramped in spaces much too small,
like a plant that needs a bigger pot,
and so gets choked and dies.
My bones are cramped tonight.

We must get there soon.
We must get there soon.

Mama

I dozed off nursing Jenny,
and Elizabeth was here,
covering me,
taking Jenny to her crib.

Sometimes I think Elizabeth practices,
this strong young girl,
in case she someday
bears this weight alone.

The children would be safe in her good care.

Elizabeth

I carry Jenny to her crib,
peace on her face.
Mama looks weak
and I grow afraid.

I am not so strong
as they think I am.

Alma

When we stopped today,
a travelling missionary appeared along the way.
He told of Indians he lived with,
and of the great river called the Rushing Waters.
Before he left,
he put two teaspoonfuls of precious sugar in my cup.

I think that I shall taste its sweetness
for many years to come.

Peter and Jeremy

"Let's pretend we're jungle animals,
a lion stalking a gazelle."

    "I'll be the lion!"

"I'll be the lion!"

    "I'll be the lion!"

"We'll take turns."

    "Me first!"

"Me first!"

Peter, Alma, and Mama

Peter:
"Why did Jenny scream so in the night?
I do not think I slept at all."

>Alma:
>"It was the monster Harold after her,
>but she escaped unharmed."

>>Mama:
>>"More teeth are coming,
>>that is all.
>>More teeth are breaking through."

Peter:
"Good thing that growing
doesn't hurt that much."

>>Mama:
>>"Sometimes it does."

Mama

We will need sweaters for the cold days to come.
The yarn tangles as I roll it into a ball
in the bouncing of this wagon.

The children are all asleep now,
save Joseph who draws.

I should sleep, too.
Jenny will waken early,
ready to nurse.
But there is no real sleep for me
on these bumpy, rolling roads.

Papa

Crossing the prairie
is not the stuff of cowards.
The young ones are too young
to know that they are brave.
Elizabeth and Joseph never complain,
despite their age and stirrings.

Yet it is Mary who suffers most.
Her light dims these last days,
but she says nothing.
I am afraid for her,
                My candle in the prairie darkness.

Elizabeth

When we stopped today,
I hung some clothes to dry.
John Harwood came to hold the basket
and to talk as I worked.
When his little sister, Emily,
came to get him,
he carried her piggyback to his wagon.
John's eyes are restful as a quiet river,
and he is as steady as the ground.

I hope we talk again.

Mama

Just now I turned,
    and didn't recognize Elizabeth
    hanging up the wash.
Did I sleep for years
    that she is suddenly this young woman
    standing so new in the sunlight,
        as perfect as a summer rose?

Jeremy

When we stop,
after chores,
Peter and I run
like cheetahs in a forest.

With Joseph,
it is different.
When his work is done,
he wanders into trees,
sketchbook in hand,
and stays until we leave again.

What is it
to be eighteen years of age?

Peter

They think because they're older
that they remember Benny more than I do.
They think because I laugh and run with Jeremy,
that it is easier for me.
They forget that Benjamin slept next to me
the night his fever started.
He asked could he dig for earthworms
with me tomorrow,
and I said, "Yes."
I haven't dug for earthworms since.

Mama and Alma

Mama:
"How can there be so many stockings to mend
when we do so little moving about these days?"

        Alma:
        "It is just the stocking ghosts
        that haunt your life
        so you're not bored."

Mama:
"Tonight my fingers
do not like the joke."

Mama

I was lucky.
We marry so young,
      so eagerly,
blind people crossing a carriage-filled path.

Now that I grow older,
I think it odd
that this circle we form
for the generations to come,
we fashion so young,
so blind to the beauty
of that which we create.

Jeremy and Papa

Jeremy:
"I wish the rains would stop.
For days now when we pause,
we cannot run or play.
I wish the rains would stop."

        Papa:
        "I hope to be so blessed
        during the summer of our first corn."

Alma

My stomach aches
in this bad-dream night.
Should I wake mama?
She will think of Benjamin.

Still, I need to feel the warmth of her
on this bad-dream night.

Mama

Hush, my little girl of fairy tales,
let go of your dark dreams.
Even at night,
your imagination chases you.
Your heart is racing,
and your face is hot against my hand.

You, my little girl of fairy tales,
will find magic roads to follow
in the days that will be yours.

Papa

Bessie's foot is swollen now,
and she cannot pull her share.
It will be hard for the other horses,
all day with little rest.

Oh, let it be a stone
that slows her now,
and not a disease to cripple her days.
I don't know how
we would travel the long days
without her.

Joseph

Papa says it is a stone in Bessie's foot.
But I saw his face,
and it is filled with lines.

We are so helpless
and need the things
that only luck can bring.

Alma and Papa

"Papa, what is wrong with Anastasia?"

"Who?"

"Anastasia, our ivory steed."

"You mean Bessie,
our white nag?"

"She limps behind the wagon.
How will she lead us on
into our kingdom?"

"She is worn just as we are,
weary from the long journey,
tired of the pulling.
It is just a little swelling
from the stone I removed."

"So will Anastasia
lead us on again?"

"You mean Bessie."

"When, Papa?"

"Soon, child, soon.
Maybe tomorrow."

Mama and Papa

Papa:

"I wonder after Alma.
She pretends too much
of things that are not real."

    Mama:

    "And what is real on these dusty roads?
    She has a good imagination, Samuel,
    and it will serve her well.
    We should all imagine so."

Peter

We stopped to water the horses
and Jeremy and I ran barefoot in the water.
Catching toads felt like
having a place to stay put.

Soon, Mama says.
Soon.

Mama

I wake again.
The wind is a voice tonight.

Where, where, where
are you, little boy?

Where, where, where
are you, my little red-headed boy?

PART II
ARRIVING…

Papa

And now I think I see the posts
that mark our land.
Strange after all this time
for sturdy wooden posts to look so fair.
Was it so for our great-grandparents
to first spot from water
the green of the land?

Whatever comes of this place,
it is good to be arriving.

Samuel and Mary

Samuel:
"Look Mary,
there are tall trees all around,
and a river to the south.
It will be fertile soil."

Mary:
"It looks to be a fine, fine place indeed, Samuel."

Samuel:
"And I will work hard
for all of us, my Mary."

Mary:
"You always have…"

Mama

Home.
Not even a tent,
or a shelter.
But trees at least
for shade,
and for building,
and no more days of bumping
along sandy, worn out roads.

It won't be easy here.
Samuel talks of catching rabbit today,
and I think of my own tiredness
and how will I make rabbit stew tonight.
I must find a time to rest.

Home.
I look at Peter and Jeremy and Alma laughing.
Only Joseph and Elizabeth are quieter.
They have seen more,
      and they know.
And they see Benjamin
      in my and Papa's eyes.
Home.
It is where we are.
Tonight we will bless our food

under a tree that will be a kind of home.
It will not be easy here,
but it will be ours.
Perhaps more often now,
we will laugh again
      and sing.
And stay warm in this circle
that is our family.

Home.

Joseph

How much the children dance
to see this forest place.
Jeremy and Peter and Alma and Abby throw the balls,
and they laugh already at their freedom.

Freedom.
Free to cut down trees,
       and chop wood,
       and build a cabin
       that will need constant patching
       from the wind and cold.
Free to plant the corn
that may die without the rain.
Free to struggle with only stolen moments
for my music and my drawing.

How much the children dance to see this place.

Mama

Tonight around the campfire,
there is peace.
Not the peace of silence alone,
but the peace of arriving,
the deep peace of the woods.
We sing of the old songs,
and Samuel's face,
so tense of late,
looks young and dancing in the moving flames.

For a moment,
he looks toward me,
and we seem children once again.
There are not words enough
to say how much I love this strong, dear man
who holds us in his heart.

Peter

Today Papa told me to dig earthworms.
I said, "No, Papa" and walked away.
He looked at me as if struck,
and Mama's face went stone.

He found me by the river.
"What, son?" was all he said.
And so I told him about my promise to Ben
to dig earthworms in the morning with him.
But darkness came that night for Benny,
and there would never be a morning
for Ben and me to dig again.

I never saw my Papa cry before,
and I may never see him cry again.
But by the river today,
I felt his hot tears,
and the roughness of his beard against my face,
and the trembling of his arms.
And we wept.

Together.

Papa

Peter is the one who never cried.
Even as a baby,
I recall him falling on a stump
or catching on a nettle,
and getting up, unnerved,
to right himself again.
No worries.

So now I ask myself.
Did I choose not to see his pain
in order not to stir
the hurt too deep inside of me?
Cowards know pretending
is the easy way.

Jeremy

The leaves begin to change
and Peter and Alma and Abby and Emily and me
jump into leaf piles today.
Papa says we must build quickly,
                    he fears an early frost.
Last night, after we no longer worked with him,
he still pounded nails late into the night.
Mama looks as tired worrying after him
as he looks from the work.

Mama

I forget sometimes that Benjamin is gone.
Today the baby pulled my skirt,
and I half-turned
expecting Benny's red hair and his grin.

It will always be like this,
a child stopped in time.
When the others are grown
and have children of their own,
it will be Benny who will be the baby still.

Who was never given the time he should have had
to become who he was meant to be.

Mama

I set out a few things of Benjamin's
from the old box.
A chewed-up blanket.
A wooden train car
from his first Christmas.
A frayed sock bear.

What's left behind is nothing
of the red-headed boy
who scrambled briefly through my life.

Yet today I touch these things
because they are all that I can ever hold of him.

John Harwood and Elizabeth

John:
"Come to see the woods with me, Elizabeth!
I visited there this morning,
and it is full of sweet berries
and wild apples."

Elizabeth:
"And burrs and brambles, too, I think."

John:
"We'll stay clear of those.
Come see the woods with me, Elizabeth."

Mama

We need each other's strength.

Before we left Chicago, my dear friend Catherine
gave me her finest china cup
and a leather book of verse.

She wrote: "This is for remembering
to take time for rest and words."

She meant: "This is for remembering
that I walk the roads with you."

Each day I will drink of tea and words,
but it is not so good as seeing Catherine again would be.

PART III
HOME...

Jeremy

Mama is not so pale this morning,
and Papa is whistling.
Did he used to whistle
in the days before?
I can't remember.

But Mama halfway grinned
when she heard it,
and her eyes were as shiny as new marbles.

Joseph

The banjo is unpacked now,
and its sound is so clean in these woods,
a part of the forest,
a part of the wind,
a part of the sky.

Perhaps it is that I've not heard its voice
these many, many days.

Now that I hear its clarity,
I understand.

This will be a perfect place for music.

Alma

They say if you turn yellow from the dandelions
that you are in a golden place.
Today I ran with Peter and Abby
in a field full of dandelions,
and we colored ourselves all yellow,
head to toe.

Peter said, "I think the dandelions were there
to say that we have found a golden place."

                                        I think so too.

Elizabeth

John's family will be building close to us,
a mile up the road.
He and Abby walked down today,
Emily piggybacked on John.
Abby gave me the Queen Anne's Lace
she had found along the way,
as fine as crocheted doilies.

John blushed as if they were from him.

Papa

John Harwood walked a ways today with Emily and Abby
to say hello to Elizabeth.
His face was flushed
not from the walking alone, I think to myself.
And I remember my younger days,
me with Mary.

Does Elizabeth see?
Does she know the boy's awkwardness
so bared in front of her?
Do any of them know
what it is to be a man,
standing overcome,
looking for a sign?

Mary and Samuel

Samuel:
"It is not so many years now
that Joseph and Elizabeth
will be leaving us."

    Mary:
    "It is years enough
    that I need not think of it tonight."

Samuel:
"They are birds, Mary, and,
like the birds, they must fly away."

    Mary:
    "Someday soon I will think on it,
    but not tonight, Samuel.
    Not tonight."

The Family Campfire

Jeremy:
"I haven't heard you talk all week of princesses, Alma."

Alma:
"We have arrived in the magic kingdom,
and now I dream of what's to be."

Elizabeth:
"Mother, are you tired?
Can I brew some tea?"

Mama:
"No, I just rest my eyes.
I feel stronger
than in many, many days."

Papa:
"And tomorrow, when the roof is finished,
we will sleep in our own home.
I sense we barely beat the frost."

Peter:
"But we beat it, Papa."

Jeremy:
"Play a song, Joseph.
Play a brand new song."

Joseph:
"Tonight I want to play of old songs.
and I will play 'Oh! Suzanna'
that Benny loved so much."

Papa:
"Your music is a gift, Joseph,
that lets you say the things we cannot."

Joseph:
"Thank you, Papa."

Mama:
"We've all been greatly blessed,
with blessings more to come.
So let's sing tonight
of days gone by,
and new days yet to come.
Let us sing tonight."

www.ingramcontent.com/pod-product-compliance
Lightning Source LLC
LaVergne TN
LVHW051226070526
838200LV00057B/4617